This book belongs to:

Luke Pajk

from The Rajewokis

August 28, 2003

Retold by Gaby Goldsack
Illustrated by Kim Blundell (John Martin & Artists)
Designed by Jester Designs

Language consultant: Betty Root

ISBN 0-75259-427-3

This is a P³ book
This edition published in 2002

P³
Queen Street House
4 Queen Street
Bath BA1 1HE, UK
Copyright © Exclusive Editions 2002

Printed in China.

Chicken-Licken

Helping Your Child Read

Learning to read is an exciting challenge for most children. From a very early age, sharing storybooks with children, talking about the pictures, and guessing what might happen next are all very important parts of the reading experience.

Sharing Reading

Set aside a regular quiet time to share reading with younger children, or to be available to encourage older children as they develop into independent readers.

First Readers are intended to encourage and support the early stages of learning to read. They present well-loved tales that children will enjoy hearing again and again. Familiarity helps children identify some of the words and phrases.

When you feel your child is ready to move ahead, encourage him or her to join in so that you read the story aloud together. Always pause to talk about the pictures. The easy-to-read speech bubbles in **First Readers** provide an excellent "joining-in" activity. The bright, clear illustrations and matching text will help children understand the story.

Building Confidence

In time, children will want to read *to* you. When this happens, be patient and give continual praise. They may not read all the words correctly, but children's substitutions are often very good guesses.

The repetition in each book is especially helpful for building confidence. If your child cannot read a particular word, go back to the beginning of the sentence and read it together so the meaning is not lost. Most importantly, do not continue if your child is tired or just needs a change.

Reading Alone

The next step is for your child to read alone. Try to be available to give help and support. Remember to give lots of encouragement and praise.

Along with other simple stories, **First Readers** will help ensure reading is an enjoyable and rewarding experience for children.

One day Chicken-Licken was in the field when an acorn fell on her head.

"Oh dear!" said Chicken-Licken. "The sky is falling. I must tell the king."

So Chicken-Licken went off to tell the king. On the way, she met Cocky-Locky.

"Where are you going in such a hurry?" asked Cocky-Locky.

"The sky is falling," said
Chicken-Licken. "I'm going to tell
the king."

"I'm coming with you," said Cocky-Locky.

On the way, Chicken-Licken and Cocky-Locky met Ducky-Lucky.

"Where are you going in such a hurry?" asked Ducky-Lucky.

"The sky is falling," said
Chicken-Licken. "We are going to tell
the king."

"I'm coming with you," said Ducky-Lucky.

On the way, Chicken-Licken, Cocky-Locky, and Ducky-Lucky met Goosey-Loosey.

"Where are you going in such a hurry?" asked Goosey-Loosey.

"The sky is falling," said
Chicken-Licken. "We are going to tell
the king."

"I'm coming with you," said
Goosey-Loosey.

15

They all walked on until they met
Foxy-Loxy.

"Where are you going in such a hurry?" asked Foxy-Loxy.

"The sky is falling," said Chicken-Licken. "We are going to tell the king."

"Ah," smiled Foxy-Loxy, who was a sly young fox. "You are going the wrong way. Follow me. I will show you the way.

So Chicken-Licken, Cocky-Locky, Ducky-Lucky, and Goosey-Loosey followed Foxy-Loxy.

Is this the way?

They walked on and on. At last they came to a cave. "Follow me," said Foxy-Loxy. "This is a shortcut."

But the cave was really
Foxy-Loxy's den.
She smiled as Cocky-Locky,
Ducky-Lucky, and
Goosey-Loosey followed her.

Chicken-Licken was about to follow
when Cocky-Locky cried out loud,
"Cock-a-doodle-doo!"

Cock-a-doodle-doo!

Chicken-Licken knew that
something was wrong.

She turned and ran away.
She ran and ran.

Chicken-Licken did not stop until she got to the barnyard. Then she looked around for her friends.

Chicken-Licken waited and waited, but her friends did not come back.

Chicken-Licken knew she was a
very lucky hen.

Chicken-Licken never did tell the king that the sky was falling. But the sky never was falling, was it?

Chicken-Licken was a very silly hen!

But she never went near a fox again.

Read and Say

How many of these words can you say?
The pictures will help you. Look back in
your book and see if you can find the
words in the story.

acorn

cave

Cocky-Locky

Chicken-Licken

Ducky-Lucky

field

Foxy-Loxy

Goosey-Loosey

hen

Titles in this series:

Chicken-Licken
Cinderella
The Gingerbread Man
Hansel and Gretel
The Three Billy Goats Gruff
The Ugly Duckling